To Brian and Mickey,
You guys are the stars of my world.

To My Parents,
For always inspiring
me to draw.

To order additional copies, please contact us.
BookSurge Publishing
www.booksurge.com
1-866-308-6235
orders@booksurge.com

My name is Charlie. Today is my first day in first grade.

This is my first-grade teacher,
Mrs. May.

And these are my first-grade classmates.

It was a beautiful day! I was in the front row, next to my best friend Freddie.

Mrs. May wrote our first lesson on the chalkboard.

I saw so many numbers.

$7 \cdot 6 =$ _____

$2 + 5 =$ _____

$8 \cdot 2 =$ _____

$5 + 3 =$ _____

$6 \cdot 9 =$ _____

It got me so scared and confused...

$2 + 2 =$ _____

$4 + 2 =$ _____

I looked around the room and everyone else was smiling and nodding.

And why is my best friend Freddie, still smiling and nodding?

I was too scared
and confused
to answer.

Instead I looked
for a place
to hide—
under
the desk,
behind the books.

I had no place to hide.
Finally, someone else yelled out the answer.

I will always be "the kid that didn't know the answer to the first question on the first day in the first grade"!

My Mom
tried to make
me feel better.
She told me stories
of how she got scared and
confused in First Grade.

My Dad told me
not to be scared—that
school is fun.

They reminded me about that time in kindergarten...

when I saw all thoses big kids and got scared and ran into the auditorium...

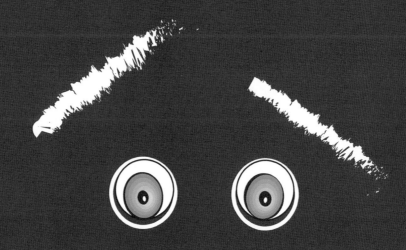

to hide.

The next day,
when I saw
those same kids by
themselves,
I didn't get scared!